Ellen's Lion

Ellen's Lion

TWELVE STORIES BY

Crockett Johnson

Alfred A. Knopf　New York

THIS IS A BORZOI BOOK PUBLISHED BY ALFRED A. KNOPF

Copyright © 1959 by Crockett Johnson

All rights reserved under International and Pan-American Copyright Conventions. Published
in the United States by Alfred A. Knopf, an imprint of Random House Children's Books,
a division of Random House, Inc., New York, and simultaneously in Canada by Random
House of Canada Limited, Toronto. Distributed by Random House, Inc., New York.
Originally published in 1959 by Harper & Brothers.

KNOPF, BORZOI BOOKS, and the colophon are registered trademarks of Random House, Inc.

www.randomhouse.com/kids

Library of Congress Cataloging-in-Publication Data
Johnson, Crockett, 1906-1975
Ellen's lion : twelve stories / by Crockett Johnson.—1st Alfred A. Knopf ed.
p.   cm.
Summary: Presents twelve episodes in Ellen's relationship with her toy lion.
ISBN 0-375-82288-7 (trade) — ISBN 0-375-92288-1 (lib. bdg.)
[1. Toys—Fiction. 2. Play—Fiction. 3. Lions—Fiction.] I. Title.
PZ7.J63162 El 2003
[Fic]—dc21
2002007288
Printed in the United States of America
February 2003
10   9   8   7   6   5   4
First Alfred A. Knopf Edition

12 Stories

CONVERSATION AND SONG

Ellen sat on the footstool and looked down thoughtfully at the lion. He lay on his stomach on the floor at her feet.

"Whenever you and I have a conversation I do all the talking, don't I?" she said.

The lion remained silent.

"I never let you say a single word," Ellen said.

The lion did not say a word.

"The trouble with me is I talk too much," Ellen continued. "I haven't been very polite, I guess. I apologize."

"Oh, that's all right, Ellen," the lion said.

Ellen sprang to her feet and jumped up and down in delight.

"You talked!" she cried. "You said something!"

"It wasn't anything that important," said the lion. "And watch where you're jumping."

"It was the way you said it," said Ellen, sitting down again. "You have such a funny deep voice!"

"I think my voice sounds remarkably like yours," the lion said.

"No, it sounds very different," Ellen told him, speaking with her mouth pulled down at the corners and her chin pressed against her chest to lower her voice. "This is how you talk."

"I don't make a face like that," said the lion.

"You don't have to. Your face is always like that," Ellen said. "It's probably why you have the kind of voice you have."

The lion did not reply.

"I didn't mean to hurt your feelings," said Ellen.

"I'm nothing but a stuffed animal. I have no feelings," the lion said, and with a sniff, he became silent.

"I like your face the way it is," Ellen said, trying to think of a way to cheer him up. "And you have got a lovely deep voice. Let's sing a song."

"What song?" said the lion.

Ellen thought of a cheerful song.

"Let's sing 'Old King Cole.'"

The lion immediately began to sing.

"Old King Cole was a merry old soul—"

"Wait," Ellen said. "Let's sing it together."

"All right," said the lion.

"*Old King Cole was a merry old soul—*" Ellen sang, and then she stopped. "You're not singing."

"*And a merry old soul was he—*" sang the lion.

"*—was he,*" sang Ellen, trying to catch up. "*He called for his pipe and he called for his bowl—*"

She realized the lion was not singing with her and she stopped again.

"*And he called for his fiddlers three—*" sang the lion.

"Can't we both sing at the same time?" Ellen said.

The lion considered the question.

"I don't think we can," he said. "Do you?"

"Let's talk," Ellen said. "It's easier."

"All right," said the lion.

"Think of something to talk about," Ellen said.

"All right," said the lion.

Ellen waited. After a minute or two she looked at the lion. He lay motionless on the floor.

"He thought so hard he fell asleep," she whispered as she left the playroom on tiptoe.

TRIP TO ARABIA

"Here comes the train," said Ellen. "It's stopping at the station. Are you ready to go?"

"Go where?" said the lion.

"To Arabia."

"That train doesn't go to Arabia," the lion said. "It

goes around in a little circle on those tracks on the floor."

"It goes through the tunnel to Arabia," Ellen told him. "And then it comes around and back to the station, by way of Greenland and Delaware Water Gap."

Sprawled out comfortably, the lion showed no inclination to go anywhere or to move at all.

"Whoooo!" said the train. "All aboard for Arabia!"

Ellen had to help the lion onto the train. She balanced him on his stomach on the roofs of the last two cars with his legs dangling on each side.

"Good-bye," said Ellen, waving her handkerchief as the train started.

The train gathered speed and headed for the tunnel. It plunged in, engine and cars and lion, and the tunnel jumped and joggled. When the last two cars reappeared from the other side the lion was not on board.

"He got off at Arabia," said Ellen.

The train continued around the tracks by way of Greenland and Delaware Water Gap. It passed Ellen and the station without stopping and it headed for the tunnel again.

This time the tunnel bounced forward as the engine drove into it and the train came to a noisy stop, with its cars off the tracks.

Ellen turned off the electric control switch and crawled around to the tunnel. She lifted it and pulled the train forward, setting the cars on the rails. She turned the tunnel upside down to examine it, pried the lion out of it, and set it over the tracks again behind the train. She put the lion back on his stomach on the last two cars and returned to the station and the control switch.

The train started smoothly and picked up speed. A family of Eskimos in Greenland were surprised to see it go by with a lion riding on it.

"Whooooo!" said the train as it approached the station and began to slow down. "Here we come from Arabia!"

But before the train came to a stop the lion's front paw hit the station roof. The roof fell off the station and the lion slid back on the tops of the cars and tumbled off the train.

With a little difficulty Ellen got the station roof back in place. Then she picked up the lion.

"Well, hello!" she said, shaking his front paw warmly. "How was your trip to Arabia? What is it like there?"

The lion refused to say a word about it.

Ellen screamed into the telephone.

"Help! There's a lion in my room!"

"Where?" said the lion.

"You!" Ellen pointed at him.

"Me? But I've always been here," the lion said. "Since the Christmas before last."

"You've got a tail with a brush on the end of it and a mane!" Ellen let her eyes grow wide. "I just realized you're supposed to be a real lion!"

"I suppose so." The lion sounded a bit annoyed. "What of it?"

Ellen stared at him with a terribly frightened expression on her face.

"What of it?" she repeated, in a trembling voice. "If you're supposed to be a real lion you're supposed to eat people when you're hungry."

"You are not in the least frightened of me, Ellen," said the lion, losing patience. "You know very well that a stuffed lion cannot be hungry and cannot possibly eat people."

"You're stuffed, so you can't be hungry." Ellen began to laugh and laugh. "That's a funny joke. Don't you see?"

The lion did not smile.

Ellen became serious too. She looked guiltily at the telephone as she set it on top of a heap of other toys.

"I don't blame you for being angry," she said. "I

should have asked you if you ate people before I called a policeman."

"You didn't call on a real telephone," said the lion.

"But I called a real policeman," said Ellen. "He'll be here any minute to take you away."

The lion said nothing. Ellen rested her chin on a fist and thought.

"Don't worry, though," she said. "I'll think of something."

"I am not worried," said the lion.

"Well, you ought to be," Ellen said. "They'll put you in the zoo, in a cage. You won't be able to get out, or go anywhere."

"I never go anywhere anyway," the lion said.

Ellen looked at the window. She jumped up and opened it wide.

"I know what," she said. "I'll tell the policeman you went away. I'll tell him you made a big leap out of the window. And you can hide."

Before the lion could argue about it Ellen snatched him up and put him in the bottom drawer of the bureau, on top of a pile of clothes. She had to press him down hard to get the drawer closed. Even so it would not close all the way. The lion's tail was caught and half of it hung down outside the drawer.

"Ouch," said the lion when Ellen finally noticed what the trouble was.

"Be quiet," she whispered. "Here comes the policeman."

"Hello, Ellen," the policeman said. "Where is the lion? I have come to put him in a cage in the zoo."

"You are too late," Ellen told him, standing in front of the bureau so he would not see the lion's tail. "The lion jumped out of the window."

"Oh." The policeman sounded disappointed. "Then I cannot put him in the zoo."

"No," said Ellen, shaking her head.

"Good-bye," said the policeman, and he went away.

Ellen opened the drawer and took out the lion. She squeezed him all over to unflatten him. But there wasn't much she could do about the kink in his tail.

"Anyway, you're safe now, thanks to me," she said as she made him comfortable on the arm of the big chair. "And you can live here happily ever after."

TWO PAIRS OF EYES

"I wish I had a drink of water," said Ellen in the middle of the night.

"Well, get one," said the lion, from the other end of the pillow.

"I'm afraid," Ellen said.

"Of what?" said the lion.

"Of things," said Ellen.

"What kind of things?" said the lion.

"Frightening things," Ellen said. "Things I can't see in the dark. They always follow along behind me."

"How do you know?" said the lion. "If you can't see them—"

"I can't see them because they're always behind me," said Ellen. "When I turn around they jump behind my back."

"Do you hear them?" asked the lion.

"They never make a sound," Ellen said, shivering. "That's the worst part of it."

The lion thought for a moment.

"Hmm," he said.

"They're awful," Ellen continued.

"Ellen," the lion said, "I don't think there are any such things."

"Oh, no? Then how can they scare me?" said Ellen indignantly. "They're terribly scary things."

"They must be exceedingly scary," said the lion.

"If they keep hiding in back of you they can't be very brave."

Ellen frowned at the lion. Then she considered what he had said.

"I guess they're not very brave," she agreed. "They wouldn't dare bother me if I could look both ways at the same time."

"Yes," said the lion. "But who has two pairs of eyes?"

"Two people have," Ellen said, staring up at where the ceiling was when it wasn't so dark. "I wouldn't be afraid to go down the hall for a drink of water if I was two people."

Suddenly she reached out for the lion, dragged him to her, and looked him in the eyes.

"Mine are buttons," he said. "They're sewn on. I can't see very well in the dark."

"Nobody can," Ellen whispered as she got out of bed. "But the things don't know that."

"How do you know they don't know?" said the lion.

"I know all about them," said Ellen. "After all, I made them up in my head, didn't I?"

"Ah," said the lion. "I said there were no such things."

"But of course there are," Ellen said. "I just told you I made them up myself."

"Yes," the lion said. "But—"

"So I should know, shouldn't I?" said Ellen, putting the lion up on her shoulder so that he faced behind her. "Stop arguing with me and keep your eyes open."

"They're buttons," said the lion, bouncing on Ellen's shoulder as she walked across the bedroom. "My eyes never close."

"Good," said Ellen, and she opened the door to the hall.

With a firm grip on the lion's tail to hold him in place she marched down the hall to the bathroom, drank a glass of water, and marched back to bed. She looked straight ahead all the way while the lion stared into the darkness behind her and during the entire trip not a single thing dared bother either of them.

DOCTOR'S ORDERS

The doctor listened to the lion's stuffing and she shook her head so sadly that her stethoscope fell off her ears.

"You're a mighty sick little lion," she said. "You'll have to stop smoking."

"You know very well that I have never smoked in my life, Ellen," said the lion, speaking in a muffled voice through his bandages.

"You are so sick you can't tell one person from another," the doctor said, reaching into a paper bag and taking out a licorice cigar. "I'm not Ellen."

"Uh?" said the lion as the cigar wedged into his mouth.

"I'm the doctor," the doctor said. "And I say you have to stop smoking. You want to get well, don't you?"

She snatched the cigar from the lion's mouth and frowned at it. She put it in her own mouth and she ate it while she took the lion's pulse and tapped his knees with a small rubber hammer to check his reflexes.

"You're going to be all right," she said. "But you'll have to take things easy for a while."

She took off the lion's bandages, bundled them up with her instruments, and closed her doctor's bag. With a BANG-BANG-BANG of the ambulance bell she drove off a hundred miles an hour through heavy city traffic. When she reached the main highway she called back over her shoulder to the lion.

"Remember, now. You have to take things easy."

The main highway widened and spread out into the prairie, where she had to use her whip on the horses to outrace a band of Indians attacking her covered wagon, and she barely made it across the Rocky Mountains, where she discovered gold.

"Gold!" she cried, and suddenly she became aware of the pirate ship sailing in close to the gold mine.

She drew her cutlass and held her own in the fight until the gang of pirates were joined by a gang of cattle rustlers and a gang of gangsters. Then she called to the lion on the end table.

"Help!"

The lion made no move to come to her aid.

"Pirates! Rustlers! Gangsters!" she shouted.

The lion didn't even look up.

"I have to take things easy," he explained.

She frowned at him.

"We were just making believe that you were sick and I was the doctor," she told him. "I'm really

Ellen. And pirates and rustlers and gangsters are after me."

Exasperated, she got out the stethoscope. Holding off the pirates and rustlers and gangsters with one hand, she listened to the lion's stuffing.

"Anyway, you're perfectly all right now," she said.

But by then the pirates and rustlers and gangsters had made off with the gold. And besides, it was lunchtime. As Ellen left the playroom she made a face at the lion.

"You always spoil everything," she said to him.

The lion continued to take things easy.

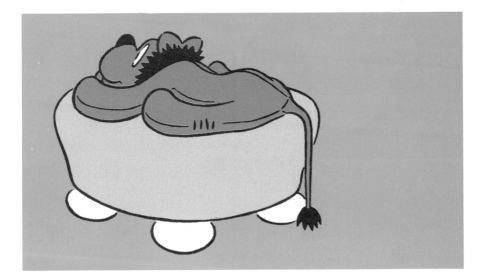

"Have you been doing any thinking about what you're going to be when you grow up?" asked Ellen.

"No," said the lion. "Have you?"

"It never occurred to me," said Ellen, raising her eyebrows. "Should I?"

"I think so," the lion said. "Why don't you? While I take a nap."

Ellen stared at him.

"I should think you'd show a little more interest," she said.

"I'm sorry," said the lion. "I didn't mean to be impolite."

"That's all right," said Ellen. "Now, suppose I think of a few suggestions. And you can decide."

"Me?" said the lion. "I can't decide. It's not my problem, Ellen."

"Of course it's your problem," Ellen said.

"Well," said the lion, sounding a little doubtful. "I'm willing to try to help."

Ellen put her chin on her fist and she began to think.

"How would it be—to be—a tiger?"

"A tiger?" said the lion.

"A real tiger. With stripes. And a big ferocious growl."

Ellen sprang about the playroom on all fours, growling ferociously.

"Your mother wouldn't like it," the lion said. "Neither would I."

"But you'd be in Africa or someplace," said Ellen. "You wouldn't live here any more."

"I certainly wouldn't," said the lion. "Not with a tiger in the house."

"You're being silly," Ellen said, frowning at him.

"Humorous," said the lion. "After all, this hardly can be called a serious conversation, can it?"

"Well!" said Ellen indignantly, and she turned her back on him. "I guess it can't!"

"Come," the lion said. "You don't really believe you can grow up to be a tiger."

Ellen's eyes opened wide and she whirled around to face him.

She laughed and laughed.

"Not me!" she shouted. "I'm going to be a lady fireman. We were talking about what you are going to be when you grow up."

"Ridiculous," said the lion.

"No it isn't," Ellen said. "You could be a tiger easily. I could cut off your mane and paint stripes on you and all you'd have to do is grow big, and learn to growl—"

"I am going to take a nap," the lion said, and he began to snore.

Ellen frowned at him.

"You're not really asleep," she said. "Your eyes are open."

"I always sleep with my eyes open," said the lion. "You know they don't close."

"I keep forgetting," Ellen said. "But why don't you want to talk about what you'll be when you grow up? Have you decided already?"

"I am not going to grow up," the lion said. "I am grown up."

"Oh," said Ellen.

For a while she sat looking at the lion, and he began to snore again.

"Tell me," she said, poking at him to make sure he was awake and not really asleep.

"What?" he said.

"Why did you ever decide to grow up to be a stuffed lion?"

But the lion definitely had lost interest in the conversation.

FIVE-POINTED STAR

A star looked down on the lion. And the star
spoke to him.

"I am your lucky star. How do I look?"

"Hello, Ellen," said the lion. "You look fine."

"It's my costume for the nursery school play," said Ellen, sitting down on the footstool and admiring the sequins on her star suit. "You knew right away that I was a star, didn't you?"

"Yes," said the lion. "I knew as soon as you said 'I am your lucky star.'"

"That's what I say when I come on in the play," Ellen said. "I say it to Gertrude Wilson. She's the queen of the carrots."

"What else do you say?" asked the lion.

"Nothing. Right after that the queen of the carrots marries Michael Kramer while we all sing 'God Bless America' and it's the end of the play."

"Then you don't come on till the end?" said the lion. "It isn't much of a part, for a star."

"I have to stand with my feet spread and my arms stretched out," Ellen said, and she got up and demonstrated. "It's very tiring."

"Oh, yes," said the lion sympathetically. "It must be."

"Anyway, I have the best costume," said Ellen. "Michael Kramer is king of the rabbits and he has a kind of bunny suit. But the other kids just stand around with vegetables on their heads. They're supposed to be vegetables, you see."

"It sounds like a very interesting play," said the lion.

"It is," said Ellen. "You ought to see it."

"I haven't been invited," said the lion.

Ellen thought.

"All the seats are for the mothers and fathers," she said.

"I understand," the lion said. "And, anyway, I have something else to do today."

"You're not doing anything," Ellen said. "You're just lying on the floor."

"That's something," said the lion.

"I'll invite you," said Ellen. "I'll hold you during the play."

"But you're in the play," said the lion.

"So will you be," Ellen said, and she swooped down on him, picked him up, and rushed off with him. "I'll tell my mother you're going to be in it."

The door slammed behind her.

A few minutes later the door opened and Ellen came in again, frowning, and still carrying the lion. She set him down in the big chair.

"I'm sorry you can't be in the play," she said.

"That's all right," said the lion. "Besides, there was one argument your mother didn't think of."

"What was that?" said Ellen.

"If you held me in one of your arms you'd only have four points."

"That's right," Ellen said, after thinking about it. "Nobody would know I was a star."

"Nobody would know," the lion said. "And everybody would miss the point of the play."

"It starts at three o'clock," said Ellen. "I have to go now."

"Good-bye," said the lion.

"I'll tell you all about it when I get back," Ellen said from the doorway.

"I'll be waiting to hear about it," said the lion. "Good luck."

Ellen left, walking with her arms stretched out and with her feet spread, like a star.

THE TWO STATUES

"What are you making, Ellen?" asked the lion, suppressing a yawn.

"Statues," Ellen told him, without looking up from the modeling clay.

"Statues of whom?"

"Just statues." Ellen pointed at two figures, one tall and thin and the other short and fat, and set

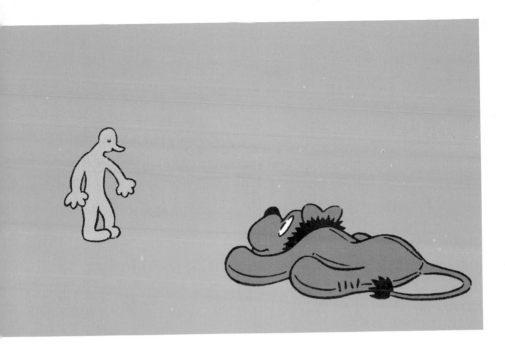

them facing the lion. "Don't they look like statues?"

"No," said the lion. "Crude figurines perhaps, not statues."

The tall figure let his head fall slightly to one side. He looked at the lion as he spoke.

"Nevertheless, I am a statue."

"See?" said Ellen, making a face at the lion. "He said so himself. He is a statue."

"A statue of whom?" the lion said. "A statue has to be a statue of somebody."

"That's right," said the statue, tossing his head farther to the side. "I am a statue of General Jones."

The head of the other statue dropped forward on his fat chest in a nod.

"And I am a statue of Admiral Smith."

Ellen straightened up their heads with her thumbs.

"The tall one is a statue of General Jones," she said. "And the short one is a statue of Admiral Smith."

"A statue has to be a statue of somebody," the lion repeated. "Who in the world are General Jones and Admiral Smith?"

The statue of Admiral Smith bowed from his fat waist.

"I am General Jones," he said.

The tall statue of General Jones bowed lower.

"I am Admiral Smith."

"They are statues of each other," Ellen explained to the lion. "Admiral Smith is a statue of General Jones and General Jones is a statue of Admiral Smith."

At the mention of their names both statues bowed again, so low that Ellen had to grab them to stop them from falling forward. As she straightened them up their legs bent and they broke into a slithering sort of jig. Despite Ellen's grasp on each of them they continued to dance. They hopped and leapt and bounced all over the place.

"That's enough," said Ellen, whose arms were getting a bit tired trying to hold them. "Statues are not supposed to dance."

Both statues kept on dancing and the Admiral began to sing.

"Oh, I am a statue of General Jones," he sang, in time to the dancing.

"Oh, I am a statue of Admiral Smith," sang the General.

"And he is a statue of me!" they sang, pointing at each other.

"Statues are not supposed to sing, either," said Ellen, turning to the lion. "Are they?"

"I would prefer it if they didn't," said the lion. "I'm thinking."

In the middle of their dance the General and the Admiral stopped abruptly and, with a final sagging shrug, they became motionless and silent.

"What were you thinking about?" Ellen asked the lion.

For a few moments before he spoke the lion stared at the tall thin Admiral who was a statue of General Jones and at the short fat General who was a statue of Admiral Smith.

"If they are statues of each other why don't they look like their statues?"

"Why don't their statues look like them, you mean," Ellen said, wiping clay from her hands.

"Well, yes," the lion agreed.

"Because I'm not a very good modeler," said Ellen.

"Oh," said the lion.

The lion lay stretched out on the soft arm of the big chair. Ellen sat on the footstool and stared at him silently for several minutes before she spoke, in her saddest voice.

"You poor thing."

"Me?" said the lion.

"Yes," Ellen said to him, and she gently stroked his imitation fur. "From now on I'm going to be very kind to you."

"Are you?" the lion said. "Why?"

"Because you're a poor sad old lion."

"I'm not old," said the lion.

"You're not new, either," said Ellen, looking at two places where the lion's seams were coming apart and at the stain, that never quite had washed out, from the time he fell off Ellen's head into her plate of tomato soup.

"And I certainly am not sad," said the lion.

"You don't look happy," Ellen said.

"I'm not," said the lion.

"Don't you have to be one or the other?" said Ellen. "I do. Right now I'm being very sad, in case you didn't notice."

"You've made it plain," the lion said.

"I'm sympathizing with you. Because you looked so sad—"

"I'm not sad!" said the lion.

"You're angry," Ellen said. "I've upset you—"

"I am never angry," said the lion. "I am never upset. For that matter, I am never in a good humor either. All this talk of sympathy for my feelings is silly, Ellen. I'm a stuffed animal."

"I know," said Ellen, sighing. "That's the saddest part of all."

"Sentimental nonsense!" said the lion, and as Ellen stared at him with eyes that were filling with tears, he went on rapidly. "I'm never sad and never happy, never hungry or never full, never foolish or clever, or good or bad, or this or that, or anything else you imagine me to be—"

"You poor thing," Ellen said, slowly shaking her head. "You haven't any mother, either, have you?"

"What has that got to do with it?" said the lion.

"It just occurred to me," said Ellen, with a sob.

"Now you are being ridiculous," the lion said. "You know stuffed animals don't have mothers. We don't need them."

"You're so brave about everything," Ellen said, dabbing at her tears with her handkerchief.

"I'm neither brave nor cowardly," said the lion.

"Your admiration is as foolish as your pity—"

"All right," said Ellen, wiping away the last of her tears and opening a picture book. "I won't sympathize with you any more if you don't like it."

"I neither like it nor dislike it—"

"Oh, be quiet," Ellen said, without looking up from her book.

She was reading a very sad story about a little tree that was lost in the woods. She read it right to the end without saying another word.

FAIRY TALE

Once, twice, and thrice the beautiful fairy waved her wand and, before she spoke, she took another bite of muffin covered with raspberry jam.

"There," she said. "Now the evil charm the wicked witch put on you can be broken. When the princess gets here you won't have to be a beast any more."

"What did you say?" said the lion. "Don't talk with your mouth full, Ellen."

"Who's Ellen?" said the beautiful fairy. "I'm your fairy godmother."

"I thought you were Ellen pretending to be an Indian," said the lion. "I saw that arrow in your hand—"

"It's a magic wand," said the fairy, putting the feathered shaft on the floor in front of the lion for him to see it plainly. "I have to disappear now. Good-bye."

"Good-bye," said the lion.

The beautiful fairy disappeared.

"Look!" said the invincible knight. "An arrow!"

"It's a magic wand," said the lion.

"Don't you know an arrow when you see one?" said the invincible knight, picking it up, tasting its rubber tip and finding it poisoned, and then rushing to the window. "Infidels! Infidels are attacking the castle!"

"Oh?" said the lion.

"The wicked witch is leading them," the knight reported, eating jam and muffin as she surveyed the besieging army across the wide moat. "But I'll save the castle. Don't worry, prince."

"Prince?" said the lion.

"You're the king's son the witch put the charm on," the knight explained. "And I'm the invincible knight. I'm on your side."

"Good," said the lion.

The arrow sailed out of the window, like a spear. And then, with no warning or explanation of any kind, the invincible knight clutched at her throat and fell back dying.

"The wicked witch is dead," she gasped. "The arrow I threw at her went right through her mean old heart and the infidels all ran away. The castle is saved."

Stuffing the last of the muffin and raspberry jam in her mouth, the knight sprawled out flat on her back and died.

"But what happened to you?" said the lion.

"Don't you remember anything?" said the dead

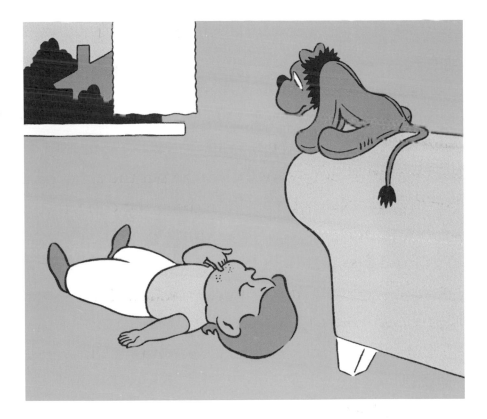

knight, rolling onto her stomach and frowning at the lion. "Don't you remember when I tasted the arrow to see if it was poisoned?"

"Oh, yes, of course," said the lion. "But I'm glad you recovered."

"The invincible knight died," said the lovely princess, clambering to her feet. "I'm the princess. You know, the one who is going to break the evil charm and change you from a beast into a handsome prince."

"How?" said the lion.

"By kissing you, of course," said the lovely princess, picking up the lion from the floor and holding him out at arm's length.

"You have jam on your face," said the lion.

"That won't matter," the princess said, and she kissed the lion and held him tight against her. "Now you're a handsome prince and we can be wed and live happily ever after."

But when the lovely princess released the handsome prince from her embrace he changed right back into a stuffed beast and fell to the playroom floor, bouncing under a red fire truck.

"I have to go down to the back yard and get that arrow I threw out of the window," said Ellen.

MOUNTAIN CLIMB

"Are you by any chance a mountain lion?" Ellen asked.

"No," said the lion.

"How do you know?" said Ellen. "Have you ever tried climbing a mountain?"

"No," said the lion.

"Wouldn't you like to be the first lion to climb the highest mountain in the world?" said Ellen, dragging a skipping rope out from under a pile of toys.

"No," said the lion.

"The trouble with you is you have no ambition," Ellen said. "You just lie there on the floor, not even moving. You don't even move your mouth when you talk. Don't you want to be famous?"

Before the lion could say "no" again, she wrapped one end of the rope around his stomach and the other end around her waist.

"Mountain climbers always tie themselves together in case one of them falls," she explained. "Anything you want to know about mountain climbing, just ask me. Have you any more questions?"

"No," said the lion.

So he and Ellen set off for the highest mountain in the world. They arrived at the foot of it and Ellen pointed up toward the summit.

"It doesn't look so high because the top is in the clouds," she said. "But be very careful."

With the lion behind her Ellen reached the cushioned seat of the mountain and without pausing she began the next part of the climb. Kneeling on top of a broad padded arm she looked over her shoulder at the lion.

"Are you out of breath?" she called. "We can rest here awhile."

She swung around on the top of the arm and, as she sat down, she noticed that the lion suddenly had disappeared. Looking over her shoulder again, she saw him, dangling on the rope over the outside of the arm.

"You slipped off the edge of the cliff," she said, pulling him up by the rope and sitting him beside her. "You'd better go first the rest of the way."

The lion went first and, with Ellen close behind him to give him a hand when he needed it, he accomplished the long difficult climb. There he was, balanced precariously, on the summit of the highest mountain in the world.

"Good work," Ellen said, drawing herself up on her knees beside the lion and giving him a pat on the head.

Over he went again, off the back of the mountain. This time the rope pulled loose and he landed with a bounce on the playroom floor.

"I told you to be careful," Ellen shouted, looking down at him from the top of the mountain. "Are you very dead?"

"No," said the lion.

"Good. Then you're famous," said Ellen, and she climbed down the mountain and took the lion by the paw. "Let's go and see the mayor and get your medal."

After the mayor presented him with a gold medal for being the first lion to climb the highest mountain in the world, the lion sat on the table at a banquet where a glass of milk and pieces of a cupcake were served and a thunderous ovation rang out. The hand-clapping and cheering went on even after the lion fell off the table and lay on the floor again and it contin-ued until everyone forgot who the applause was for or what it was he was famous for having done.

THE NEW SQUIRREL

Ellen came in with a brand-new squirrel, holding him high over her head.

"I just got him for my birthday," she said. "Isn't he adorable?"

"Is he?" the lion said.

Ellen cuddled the squirrel to her.

"Hasn't he got the most appealing expression?"

"Has he?" said the lion.

"And wait till you hear this," said Ellen, inserting a key in the squirrel's side and twisting it around and around. "Listen."

The squirrel began a song but not at its proper beginning, and it came out of him in a tinkling voice that carried only the tune, not the words.

"—one-horse open sleigh-ay, jingle bells, jingle bells, jingle all the way . . . oh what fun it is to ride in a one-horse open sleigh-ay, jingle bells—"

"Isn't he wonderful?" Ellen said.

"He has a music box inside of him," the lion said.

"I know," said Ellen, holding the squirrel against her cheek, listening to him, and stroking his fur. "That's what's so wonderful."

"Machinery," said the lion. "Just something to get out of order."

"You're jealous," Ellen said. "You haven't got a music box in your stomach."

"Neither have you," said the lion. "I don't think it is a matter to give either of us any great cause for envy."

"I swallowed a whistle once," said Ellen.

"I remember," the lion said. "And it was quite a calamity. The doctor came. Your mother and father and I were up all night."

"Were you here then?" Ellen said. "It was long ago. I was little."

"I was here long before that," said the lion. "Even before you had the measles. Remember? I stayed in bed with you the whole time."

"—sleigh-ay, jingle bells, jingle bells, jingle all the—"

The squirrel stopped tinkling. Ellen reached for the key and wound him up again while she stared at the lion.

"You might have caught the measles," she said.

"Your mother disinfected me," the lion said. "It took three days on the clothesline in the sun for me to dry. My fur faded."

"—*way*. . . *oh what fun it is to ride in a one-horse open sleigh-ay, jingle bells*—"

Ellen carried the squirrel, tinkling merrily again, to a corner of the room and set him on the floor.

"The lion and I are talking about things from long ago," she explained, leaving him and returning to the lion. "When you were disinfected it must have been as bad as the time we had to put you in the washing machine after you fell in the mixing bowl."

"It was much the same sort of experience," said the lion.

"I remember when we pulled you out of the brownie batter," said Ellen, suddenly laughing. "It was very funny."

"It's funny now," said the lion. "Looking back on it."

In the corner of the room the squirrel tinkled on.

"Remember when Sarge Thompson kidnapped you and took you to his kennel?" Ellen said.

"You cried," said the lion.

"But I rescued you," said Ellen.

"I was proud of you," said the lion.

"—*bells, jingle bells, jingle all the way . . . oh what*—"

The squirrel tinkled to a stop. Nobody noticed. Nobody wound him up again. Ellen and the lion were busy talking over old times.

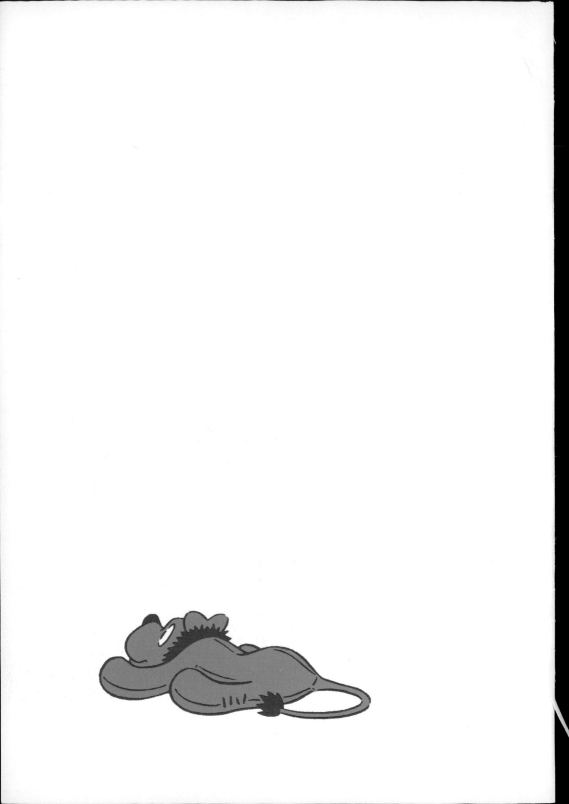